Ugly Duckling

Illustrated by Michael Jaroszko

sequoia
children's publishing

Mother duck was very happy today. Six of her eggs had hatched. She now had six yellow, fluffy ducklings to take care of! They all watched as the last egg began to hatch. Little by little, the newest duckling pecked his way out.

But this little duckling wasn't yellow like the others.

"He's an ugly duckling," whispered a brother.

"Hush, now. He's not a bit ugly—just different," said his mother. She tucked the new duckling under her wing.

The next day, the mother took her ducklings
swimming. They all loved the water, especially the
gray duckling. He glided gracefully across the pond.

But when it came time to walk across the muddy
bank, he wasn't as graceful. He landed on his bottom
with a big, muddy *splat!*

The other ducklings laughed at him. He sadly
swam away to hide in the reeds. Just then, two
magnificent birds floated past. They were white,
with lovely long necks.

"I'll never be so beautiful," thought the duckling.
He began to swim back to his mother, but a man picked
him up from the reeds!

"You poor little thing," said the man. "You are all alone." The man brought the duckling to his farm. He was kind, but the farm animals were not so kind.

"What sort of duck are you?" asked the chicken.

"An ugly one!" laughed the cat.

The duckling spent a lonely winter at the farm. He missed his family.

When spring returned, he found his way back to the pond. When his mother saw him, she smiled proudly. The duckling waited for his brothers and sisters to tease him, but they did not.

Nearby, he saw the same magnificent white birds he had seen the year before.

"They're beautiful, aren't they, Mother?" asked the duckling.

"Yes, they are beautiful swans," said his mother, "like you."

The duckling looked at his reflection in the
water. Looking back at him was a handsome swan!
He glided over to the other swans, knowing that
they would welcome him as a friend.

~◦~ **The End** ~◦~

New Words

duck
(ducks)

Duck is the common name for a large group of aquatic birds. They live all over the world, in both fresh and salt water. The name duck comes from an Old English word that means "to dive," probably because ducks feed with their heads below water and their bottoms in the air! This is called dabbling. Male ducks are called drakes; females are called ducks or hens. Baby ducks, called ducklings, are covered in soft, cuddly feathers.

graceful
(gracefully)

Graceful describes movement that is easy and beautiful. A swan is considered graceful because it swims and flies with ease and holds its neck in a pretty S shape. The opposite of graceful is clumsy. The Ugly Duckling might have been graceful on the water, but he was clumsy on the land, and he fell on his bottom!

swan
(swans)

Swans are much larger than ducks or geese and have longer necks. They never live in tropical areas, but they can be found in cooler climates across the world. Male swans are called cobs; females are called pens. Baby swans are called cygnets. Just like duckling means "little duck," cygnet means "little swan." It's based on the French word for swan: *cigne*. How fancy is that?

tuck
(tucks, tucked, tucking)

Tuck means to put into a snug and safe place. Mamma duck tucks the Ugly Duckling under her wing so he will feel safe from the other ducklings who are teasing him. If someone tucks you into bed, they push the covers in around you so you feel warm and safe.

glide
(glides, glided, gliding)

To **glide** is to move smoothly and quietly. When the story says the swans glide across the pond, it means they swim without splashing or making a lot of noise. Glide also means to fly slowly through the air without a lot of flapping, relying on the wind to carry you along. If you throw a paper airplane, it glides back to the ground.

bank
(banks)

A **bank** is the raised land along a body of water, like a lake or river. The bank slopes toward the water and is often muddy or wet, which can make it slippery (as the Ugly Duckling found out). Don't put your money in this bank unless you want it to get all soggy!

Story Discussion

After you are done reading the story, think about how the duckling was treated before and after he became a swan. Be sure to look back at both the pictures and the words. Now it's time to answer these questions and talk about what the story means to you. After you read each question, choose the best word or think of your own.

1.) Look at the beginning of the story. Which word describes the duckling's mother?

Loving   Curious

Embarrassed   Something else?

2.) Look back at when the duckling first went to the pond. How do you think he felt after getting covered in mud?

Sad   Playful

Bored   Something else?

3.) Look back to when the duckling was at the farm. What word describes how the other animals treated him?

Nice   Mean

Generous   Something else?

4.) Look at the end of the story. How did the duckling feel once he realized he was a swan?

Confused   Happy

Shy   Something else?

5.) Look at the end of the story when the Ugly Duckling was reunited with his mother. Which word describes how his mother felt about the Ugly Duckling after he became a swan?

Loving   Scared

Proud   Something else?

~∽৬∽∙∘ What's Different ∘∙∽৬∽~

The Ugly Duckling fell in the mud! But there's a lot more going on than just that. Can you find 10 differences between the two pictures? (Answers on page 21)

Did You Know?

There are lots of different names for a group of ducks. A group of flying ducks is called a flock. Waddling ducks are called a brace or a badling. Swimming ducks are called a raft, team, or paddling. Swan groups don't have quite as many names: Flying swans are called a flock or a wedge. Swans on the ground are called a bevy, bank, or herd. Why do duck and swan groups need so many names? You'll have to ask them!

Both ducks and swans migrate, which means they live in one place during the summer, and then fly somewhere warmer for winter. In North America, many swans nest in the arctic for the summer and fly south to warmer areas for the winter. Some swans don't migrate at all. They stay put year round as long as there is enough food. Ducks live in a lot of different places, but if it gets cold, most fly south for a winter vacation. Some people do the same thing. They fly south during the cold winter. Their nickname is snowbirds!

Swans usually find a mate by the time they are two years old and stay with them for life. And that can be a long time! Swans can live to be 30 years old, which is three times longer than ducks.

The *Ugly Duckling* was written by Hans Christen Anderson in 1843. He wrote many other fairy tales you might know, including *The Little Mermaid*, *The Emperor's New Clothes*, *The Princess and the Pea*, and dozens of others. He also wrote plays, travel journals, and poems. Hans Christen Anderson was a busy guy! His stories have been made into countless movies, plays, music, television shows, and cartoons.